My Uncle Bob

Written By William Arnold
Illustrated By Remi Bryant

Illustrations and book design by Remi Bryant
www.playpenpublishing.com

ISBN: 978-0-9994380-4-6

My name is William Stevens. This story is about my uncle Bob. He's my best friend and the greatest role model in the world. As most stories go, there is happiness and then there is sadness in every family.

I was 6 when my father passed away. After that, it was just my mother and me. I missed my father and my mother said I cried a lot! There is a saying that says after the storm, the sun will shine again. For me, that sunshine was my uncle Bob. With a heart of gold and so much understanding, Uncle Bob took me under his wing, and he became my very best friend. Uncle Bob was 40 years old. He was 3 feet and 6 inches tall.

He always wore a black derby that he tilted on the side of his head. Plus, there was always a cigar in the corner of his mouth. Some say he dressed like an undertaker because he would always wear a black suit, white shirt, skinny black tie, shiny shoes and that black derby.

My grandmother asked Uncle Bob to take care of me. Because my mom had to work, he took me to school on the first day. Uncle Bob drove a blue bug. A bug is a nickname for the little Volkswagen Beetle car. He had to sit on 4 piles of pillows and wore a special shoe that helped him reach the pedals. To see him driving was a masterpiece in itself! Half the time it looked like no one was driving! It was the first day of school and somehow we got there late. I don't think my uncle knew how to get to the school because it was newly built. I think it was built a year ago. So as Uncle Bob would say, "I'm not lost, just a little confused."

The bell was ringing for all the students to be in class. It was my first day and I didn't know where my class was.

Down the hall we went. Mrs. Hill, the Health Education teacher came up behind us. She was about 5 feet, 11 and 1/2 inches tall and she walked really quietly.

All she could see was cigar smoke coming from a 3 foot 6 inch tall student. Mrs. Hill walked up to my uncle and THWACK! She popped him in the back of his head, grabbed his derby and snatched that cigar out of his mouth. "To the principal's office young man!" she yelled as she grabbed him by the back of his collar and raised him up to his tippy-toes.

Uncle Bob snatched away from her grip, whipped around and growled, "What are you doing lady? Let me go! I'm a grown man!" Startled by the gruff voice, Mrs. Hill dropped her hold and said, "That's why you are so short! Smoking stunted your growth!" Uncle Bob looked at me and said, "What are you laughing at?" We got everything straight and Principal Wood told Uncle Bob to walk me to my class. He wanted him to know where my class was too. Uncle Bob had a note from the office to give my teacher. Before he had a chance to give it to my teacher she said, "You two students can take those two seats. She pointed to the front of the classroom. My uncle said, "Lady, I'm bringing my nephew to class. I'm a grown man." The kids all laughed out loud. Then, the teacher asked, "What do they call you dwarf or midget?" He replied, "If it's any of your business lady, they call me Mr. Bob. My nieces and nephews call me Uncle Bob and that is it lady. Thank you and have a nice day at school."

When I returned home after school, Grandmother asked, "How was your day Buddy?" That's what Grandmother called me, her "Little Buddy". I told her what happened and she smiled and said, "Wash your hands and get ready to eat your dinner." My mother worked her full time job plus a part time in order to make ends meet. So I stayed at my grandmother's house until she came home. Most of the time, I just stayed overnight with Grandmother.

Uncle Bob was coming home from work and there was a new family, the Parkers, that had just moved next door. They had a seven-year-old girl named Jean. Jean was playing outside when she saw Uncle Bob get out of the car. Jean said, "Little boy, ask your mother if you can come out to play." Uncle Bob bit down on the cigar in the corner of his mouth and growled, "Didn't you see me drive that car?" Wide-eyed Jean asked, "How did you do that? Are you going to ask your mother if you can come out and play?" My uncle scowled and just unlocked the door and came into the house.

He said to me, "That little girl wants to know if you want to come out and play." I was peaking through the curtains, so I knew what she said to him. I just laughed and went outside to play with her.

The next day Jean and I rode the school bus and sat together. She was in the second grade and I was in the first grade. Jean told me that she was coming over to my house after school. She said she had to finish her homework first and then we could play. Around 5 o'clock, she knocked on the door and Uncle Bob opened it. Jean said , "Hi little boy. I didn't know William had a brother." She just started talking non-stop. "Why didn't you go to school today? Were you sick? Where is William? Oh, there he is." Jean greeted William and said, "Your brother doesn't talk much. Do you think he wants to play?" Uncle Bob was going to say something to Jean. Jean said to me "That's ok. I'll just play with you. He can stay inside. He doesn't talk much does he? He'll be ok right?"

When I came back into the house Uncle Bob said, "Did you tell that motor mouth little girl how old I am?" I said no and he asked, " Why did she do all that talking? Does everybody in New Jersey talk like that? I didn't get a word in at all!" I just did what Jean said and we played and had a good time. School was always fun with her around.

Summer came around and we were out of school. One morning I looked out my bedroom window and saw a truck at Jean's house. I ran down the stairs and asked my grandmother what was going on over there. She said, "It looks like a moving truck." I ran back upstairs and woke up Uncle Bob. He would find out what was going on. Uncle Bob put on his clothes and we were quickly off to Jean's house. We ran like we were going to a fire!

Jean's father Colonel Parker was an important man in the Marine Corps. When the military gave an order to move, you had to be ready quick! His orders were moving him and his family to Germany. He told us, "I am sorry but it happened overnight. I know you are a good friend to my daughter." Jean and her family got into the truck and drove off. I was stunned! I just stood there and watched until the truck disappeared. I felt like I had been punched in the stomach. I just walked away with my head down. I thought that if I didn't watch them drive away, they wouldn't disappear like that.

Uncle Bob put his hand on my shoulder and said, "I'm going to change my clothes and we are going to the river fishing hole. So go dig some worms." I told him I didn't know how to fish. He said, "That's why Uncle Bob is here to teach you. I'll make sure that I'll never leave you. Everything will be ok. You'll see." So to the fishing hole we went. I was still a little sad but I would be all right because Uncle Bob was by my side.

He showed me how to put the worm on the hook. Hook it through the body then wrap it around with a little loop. Don't forget to leave a little dangle at the head and tail ends. With a worm on the hook, Uncle Bob tossed out his line.

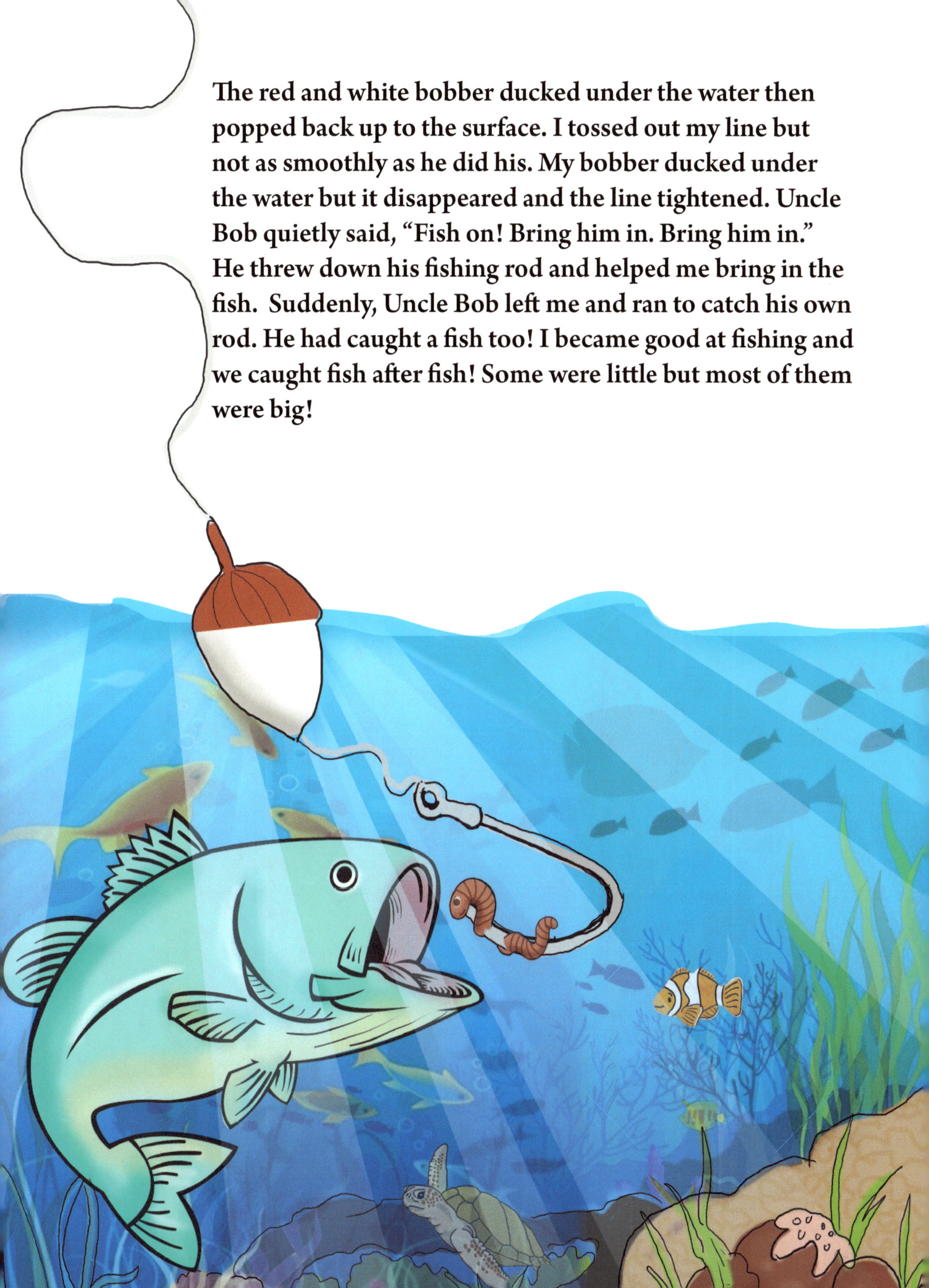

The red and white bobber ducked under the water then popped back up to the surface. I tossed out my line but not as smoothly as he did his. My bobber ducked under the water but it disappeared and the line tightened. Uncle Bob quietly said, "Fish on! Bring him in. Bring him in." He threw down his fishing rod and helped me bring in the fish. Suddenly, Uncle Bob left me and ran to catch his own rod. He had caught a fish too! I became good at fishing and we caught fish after fish! Some were little but most of them were big!

Uncle Bob asked me if I could swim. Even though I said no, he just pushed me into the water. I was in a panic and I screamed, " I said NO! I can't swim. I can't swim!" Uncle Bob laughingly said, " Well just stand up." He jumped in to the water and it almost came up to his chin. He was three and a half feet tall. He smiled and said, "I'm going to teach you how to swim." Man, could my uncle swim! Under the water and back to the top! He flew and you wouldn't believe it unless you were there. What a swimmer! We fished and swam all day long.

Uncle Bob and I had a great time. I still missed Jean but as always my uncle Bob was my hero and best friend. The next day he told me he had to take off from work for a week. He asked what I wanted to do because he took a vacation just so he could have fun with me. My mother thanked him for being my sunshine.

One day, Uncle Bob told me that we were going to the Senior Citizens Home. We were teaching the residents how to swim. I didn't know he was a swim instructor. They were always excited to see Uncle Bob. The old men had swim trunks pulled up to their chests and the old ladies had brightly colored flowers in their swimming caps. Everyone had their towels draped around their shoulders like super hero capes. They all looked forward to swim class time.

The old folks loved me just as much as Uncle Bob. We all had a great time and I got kisses, food, toys and money! They even gave me ice cream and cake! Man my uncle was great. After swimming, most of the swim students were ready for a nap until suppertime. Uncle Bob put on his derby hat and popped in an unlit cigar. We left quietly.

Next, we were off to City Park. To get there, we had to go over the Gilmerton Bridge. It's an old bridge that the city of Chesapeake, Virginia was working on. Suddenly a lady and a little girl quickly drove around us! They were driving fast and recklessly. The bridge was going up and Uncle Bob said, "I wonder why she is driving like that?" Then, she began to drive faster. Uncle Bob said, "The bridge is half way up! She's not going to make it!"

She drove over the opened bridge at top speed and her car flew into the air. The wheels were spinning and the car went off the bridge and down, down into the water they went. They sunk down deep! First the front wheels sank and then all we could see was the trunk of the car. All the people couldn't believe it. They knew that something very bad happened to the lady and her daughter. The water was really deep and all the ships, tugboats and yachts drove through there on their way to the ocean. It was at least 50 to 100 feet deep. My uncle saw everything and while everyone was looking shocked and screaming for help, he sprang into action!

I looked and Uncle Bob was taking off his hat, tie, shirt, pants and shoes. He even spat out his cigar at the same time. There was a crane operator working on the bridge. My uncle asked the operator if he could lower the crane boom down in the water. The crane operator and a crew member named Leslie Arnold lowered it and said good luck sir. By the time the bridge operator had called 911, no one knew there was a super hero already there and his name was Uncle Bob. He was my hero.

The crane operator lowered the boom into the water and my uncle did one of the most perfect dives into the water. He looked like a dolphin swimming and down into the water he went. The water was very, very dark but he could see the taillights that were on. Like the speed of a shark, he caught up with them just before the boom on the crane ran out. The crane was ready to pulled the car out of the water as if it was a fish on a hook.

After my uncle swam to the car, he could see the girl waving at him and the mother was scared.

The crane operator pulled the car out of the water and my uncle was standing on the car's trunk and holding onto the boom cable. Everyone was safely put back on land.

The rescue EMTs and police started to help. The mother passed out but the scared little girl was ok. Someone put a blanket around her and they where taken to the hospital to be checked out and questioned.

The newspaper and television crews surrounded my uncle! They wanted to know about the man that saved the people's lives. Uncle Bob was a little tired so they started talking to 6 year old me. They all asked who was that man?

You know what I asked them? "You don't know? " They said, "NO!" I said, "He is my super hero, Uncle Bob! That is the way the newspaper wrote it and the television showed it on the six o'clock news. SUPER HERO UNCLE BOB!

One week later, the mother was alright. The doctors said she had a diabetic attack and fainted. Later, the little girl started going to my school. She was 6 years old. Just like me! And guess what? Her name was Jean too and she was in my class. Sometimes in life things go wrong. Always remember that the sun will shine again and things will be ok. My sunshine is my UNCLE BOB!